In memory of Tinker.
Abbeville Press

In memory of my grandfather and his dachshund,
who live on in this book.
A.L.

For Zahid and Bastian
S.L. + S.L.

This book belongs to:

_____

Be nice to this book!

Library of Congress Cataloging-in-Publication Data
available upon request

ISBN 0-7892-0071-6

First edition
2 4 6 8 10 9 7 5 3 1

PIPPO

A Little Dog
Finds a Home

A Story by Annette Langen

With Pictures by Sigrid & Sven Leberer

ABBEVILLE PRESS PUBLISHERS

NEW YORK LONDON PARIS

Allow me to introduce myself: my name is Pippo. Well, that's not exactly right. . . . Actually, my family has many different names for me! I am Lisa's "Sausage Dog," and Jenny calls me "Wiggles." When their mom pets me, my name is "Little One." But the funniest name is the one that the biggest person, called Dad, has for me. He is especially playful and always wants to romp around with me. And as soon as I do, he calls me "No-Oh-No-Ooh-That-Tickles!" Oh, and I mustn't forget Grandpa—he actually calls me "Sweetie."

As if that were a fitting name for a regal dachshund. Really, calling me "Sweetie," even though I'm the head dog.

In some ways, these people of mine are really strange:

They don't play with sticks, don't like bones or nice smells, and can't even bark.

I wonder if they'll ever learn how to behave properly.

Even so, we get along just great.

In fact, my family is very special. They saved my life in the woods! That's a long story, and I almost wish I could forget it. But if I think hard and close my eyes, I remember it just like it happened yesterday.

The story starts on a day like any other. I was playing catch with my brothers and sisters. Even our mom was playing.

Suddenly—right in the middle of our game—something grabbed me and whisked me high in the air. I heard a shriek: "Oh, it's so cute!" And another loud voice immediately replied, "Yes, it'll make a fine present for our son."

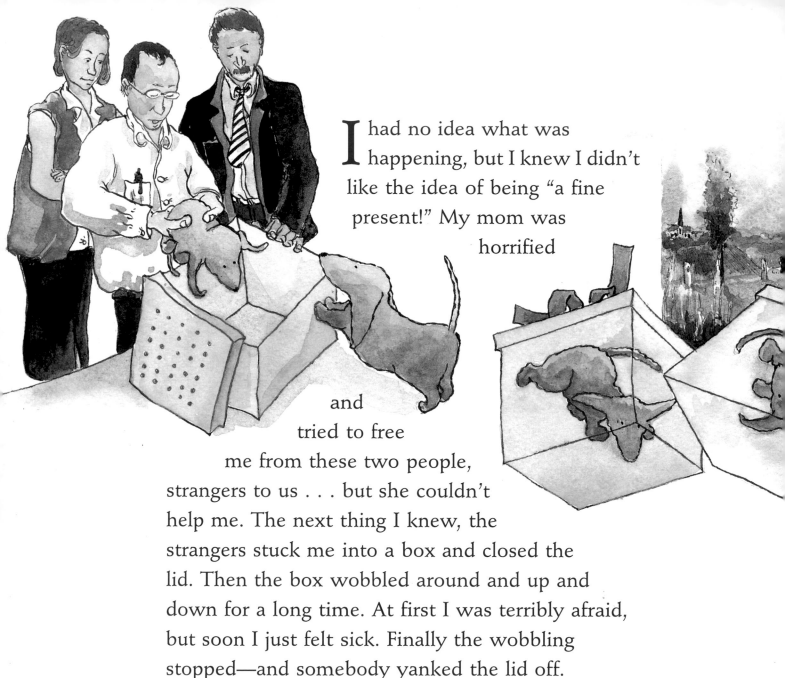

I had no idea what was happening, but I knew I didn't like the idea of being "a fine present!" My mom was horrified

and tried to free me from these two people, strangers to us . . . but she couldn't help me. The next thing I knew, the strangers stuck me into a box and closed the lid. Then the box wobbled around and up and down for a long time. At first I was terribly afraid, but soon I just felt sick. Finally the wobbling stopped—and somebody yanked the lid off.

I held my breath, pricked up my ears, sniffed, and cautiously took a look. Ah ha! Right in front of me was a young human, staring at me. In spite of my ordeal, I cordially wagged my tail and gently licked him on the hand. Did he greet me in return? No. He screamed: "Yuck! Get away!" In shock, I gave out a little bark. I heard a gasp, and somebody wailed:

"Hugo, this animal had the audacity to . . . !
Oh, this is just awful!"

A nd so began a very bad time for me—no matter what I did, it was wrong!

Inside this family's people-kennel, there was a shoe that smelled so delicious that I just couldn't resist . . .

Behind the people-kennel, there was a grassy spot they called a "garden." I can't tell you what it was good for. I did learn that I wasn't allowed to bury bones there. So I had to hide them in the sofa . . .

"Come here—now!" meant it was finally time to take a walk outside. But if I hurried she screamed: "You get away! My good coat!" Everything outside that really smelled great they called "Yuck." Puddles and damp paths in the field were "Eeew, yuck!" I couldn't understand any of this.

I wanted so much to please my new family—but they paid no attention to me. They never wanted me to fetch a stick or bark at a cat. Often they locked me up in the cellar, where there are all kinds of really scary things. At night I felt completely alone and abandoned. If I whined sadly for someone to come, after a while the cellar door would fly open. I was being released, I was overjoyed! But no! They shook me and called me "Now-You-Be-Quiet."

One day they took me to a forest in their metal monster. This was very exciting; I had never seen so many trees. Then they threw a little stick. At last a real job for me! It landed in a thicket, and I eagerly ran after it. But when I returned proudly with the stick clenched in my teeth, I was completely alone. Where had my family gone? I sniffed here and there, found their tracks, and followed the scent to the place where the metal monsters sat. There the scent ended.

The next morning I could no longer stand up. I lay there, lonely and deserted, and shivered. Suddenly I heard the voices of unfamiliar people. I began to whimper softly.

"Shhh . . . listen, it must be very nearby," a deep voice called out.

Then the branches rustled. Scared, exhausted, but hopeful, I looked up. There stood three people, one big and two small.

"Oh, look, Grandpa," they sobbed, "ooh, ooh, this poor little dog."

It sounded like a whimper—I had never heard such a thing from people! Very, very carefully, big hands picked me up.

"Don't worry, Jenny and Lisa," said the deep voice, "this little dog is going to get better."

Little hands stroked me gently. Oh, that felt good! They wrapped me in something soft and warm. I was so tired that my eyes drooped closed, and the voices whispered: "Don't be afraid, sausage dog." They carried me through the forest until we came to their people-kennel.

Jenny, Lisa, Mom, Dad,
and Grandpa saved my life back then.
They took care of me day and night, until I
could stand on my own paws once more.
Then I got a name, a collar, a little basket
with a comfy blanket, one dish for water,
and another for food. Ever since that
day I have looked after my family.

In the early morning I make sure that Dad gets out of bed on time. Nobody does this as well as I do! That's when I really do honor to my name "No-oh-no-aaah-that-tickles."

Next, I check to see that Jenny and Lisa have a good breakfast. I know that's very important for people.

After breakfast Mom puts on her white smock and we play "Who can run faster to work?" She's almost like Jenny or Lisa, the way she squeals and laughs at me! But I don't let that fool me, because Mom's smock smells like medicine. I think that she helps sick dogs, and maybe even cats, to become well again.

Soon Dad, Jenny, and Lisa ride their bikes to school. I have heard that the little people learn to make marks on paper there. Jenny and Lisa going to school I can understand, but why Dad? Doesn't he already know how to make these marks? It's strange that he still has to go to school.

When the four of them are gone, then I share a peaceful second breakfast with Grandpa. That is our secret, and I will never tell anybody! So nobody can see him, Grandpa hides behind a big crinkly paper. He calls it "checking the headlines."

When Grandpa has finished reading the paper, I go for a walk with him. Along the way I point out to him which trees and houses have the most interesting news to sniff out.

Without me along I'm sure he would miss them completely! Then we go to see if there's anything new in the city. Grandpa and I are always very busy, but I am careful to make sure that we're back home in time for lunch—wonderfully delicious smells come from the kitchen then. And of course I must be there to greet my little people when they come home. That is just about the most exciting part of the day.

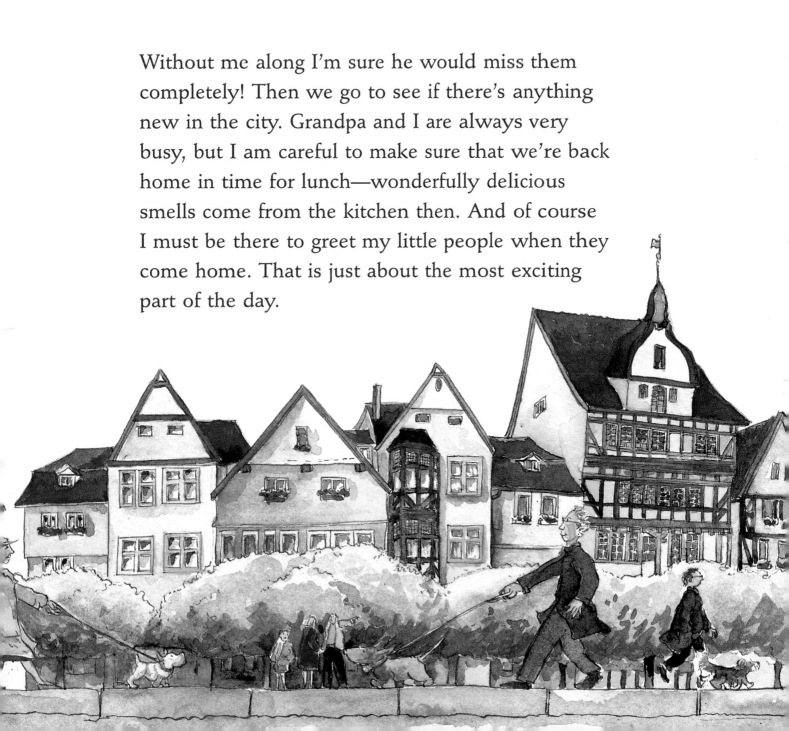

When it is so warm
that I have to pant and
the ground is much too hot for my paws,
a funny game begins: my family calls it "packing
the bags." They stuff everything imaginable into
these bags, while leaving the most important job
to me. I make sure that nothing and no one is
forgotten. We ride in their metal monster until the
air smells of salt, sand, and seaweed.

Day after day the people plunge into cold salty water and stay out there forever. Very strange behavior, but they enjoy it. As is fitting for a dachshund, I watch carefully to see that no one comes near our beach bag.

If I get really bored, I dig a good-sized hole in the sand or take a look to see if there's anything interesting in the picnic basket.

When we are back home after the big vacation,
colorful tractors drive through the fields
outside town towing machines behind them, and
then the air smells particularly good. Even my
humans go out to enjoy this air. The best thing is
that I get to ride in the basket on the front of
Grandpa's bicycle.

I really don't know why, but at this time of year Jenny and Lisa try to fly some funny birds, and they're lucky that I am always there to help them!

Those colorful birds are always really ornery, trying to get loose from their strings, but I soon make them behave.

When the leaves fall from the trees, my family has the Jenny-Lisa party. Every year I am excited all over again. First, they all constantly run back and forth between the kitchen and the hallway. The people-kennel smells like cake, and they hang pretty ribbons on the walls. A bell rings again and again, until the whole place is full of little people.

Then the big and little
people like to howl with
me. They can howl very
loudly, even though the
sounds they make are
strange, sort of like:

"Happee biiirf-day
too yoo."

After that it gets even more exciting.
The little people sit at a big table with lots
of food, a wonderful set-up, if you ask me.
Pieces of the food on the little plates, and
sometimes even creamy white cake, fall to
the floor. Yum, everything is delicious!

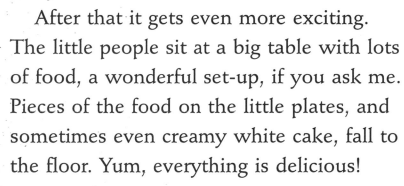

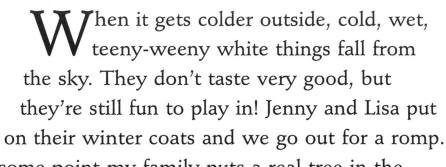

When it gets colder outside, cold, wet, teeny-weeny white things fall from the sky. They don't taste very good, but they're still fun to play in! Jenny and Lisa put on their winter coats and we go out for a romp. At some point my family puts a real tree in the people-kennel. When there are strange, wrapped things under it, then it's time for the tree party.

In the evening, when it's gotten dark, I jump into Jenny and Lisa's bed—that is our secret—and keep their paws warm.

Sometimes the three of us lie there awake for a long time looking up into the night sky and wondering how many stars there are in the heavens.

But I don't want to go up there. I will stay here forever, with my family.